STERLING CHILDREN'S BOOKS
New York

An Imprint of Sterling Publishing
387 Park Avenue South
New York, NY 10016

ISBN 978-1-4027-8346-3

Distributed in Canada by Sterling Publishing
c/o Canadian Manda Group, 165 Dufferin Street
Toronto, Ontario, Canada M6K 3H6
Distributed in the United Kingdom by GMC Distribution Services
Castle Place, 166 High Street, Lewes, East Sussex, England BN7 1XU
Distributed in Australia by Capricorn Link (Australia) Pty. Ltd.
P.O. Box 704, Windsor, NSW 2756, Australia

For information about custom editions, special sales, and premium and
corporate purchases, please contact Sterling Special Sales at 800-805-5489
or specialsales@sterlingpublishing.com.

Manufactured in China
Lot #:
2 4 6 8 10 9 7 5 3 1
08/14

www.sterlingpublishing.com/kids

SILVER PENNY STORIES

King Midas

Told by Kathleen Olmstead
Illustrated by Maurizio Quarello

There once was king named Midas. He was a good king and a kind man. However, he often did not think carefully before he spoke.

King Midas had many beautiful
things but always wanted more.
He wanted more jewels, more silver,
and more gold.

One morning, King Midas walked through his garden. He saw an old servant asleep under a tree instead of working. Rather than punish him, King Midas let him sleep.

Dionysus, a Greek god, saw King Midas do this good deed. He called out to the king. "Because you were so kind, I will grant you one wish."

Without thinking, King Midas said, "I wish everything I touch would turn into gold."

Dionysus granted him his wish.

King Midas picked a flower that was facing the sun. It was very beautiful. The flower turned into gold in his hand.

King Midas was amazed. He could turn things into gold. He picked up an apple. Gold! He touched a tree with his hand. Gold!

"My kingdom will be richer than I ever dreamed," he said. King Midas was very excited.

At dinner, King Midas picked up his fork. It turned into gold. He touched his plate, then his cup, then his food. They all turned into gold.

This worried King Midas. He was hungry but could not eat gold. He wondered if he made the wrong wish.

His daughter came in. King Midas was very excited to see her and he hugged her tightly. She turned into gold in his arms.

"Oh, what have I done?" King Midas cried out.

He tried to be careful, but sometimes he made mistakes. His guards, maid, doctors, and even his dog, all turned into gold when he touched them. His sword, books, pens, and paper, too. Nothing was safe from his touch.

With no food or water and very
little sleep, King Midas became
skinny. He looked sick.

Everyone worried about him, but they all kept their distance. No one wanted to get too close.

King Midas was lonely. He had
no one to comfort him and no one
to keep him company. He missed
his friends and servants, but he
missed his daughter most of all.

"This is not a blessing," he said.
"This is a curse! Why did I wish for such a thing? I am so sorry I spoke without thinking."

Dionysus heard King Midas. The god took pity on the king.

"I will help you," Dionysus said, "because you are truly sorry."

Just then, everything returned to normal. The plates, flowers, and forks were no longer made of gold. The guards, the maids, the doctors, and even his daughter came back to life.

King Midas hugged his daughter tightly. He was so happy. He could not turn objects into gold, but King Midas knew he was now richer than he had ever been.